The NORTH STAR

The Little Dipper

The BIG Dipper

This is NORTH

To my son, Harland

This book was written in
the first two months of
your life as I tried to make
sense of it all for you.

These are the things
I think you need to know.

HERE WE ARE

NOTES FOR LIVING ON PLANET EARTH

OLIVER JEFFERS

PHILOMEL BOOKS

OUR ★ SOLAR SYSTEM*

(ONE of ~~MILLIONS~~ ~~BILLIONS~~ TRILLIONS)

Well, hello.

Welcome to this planet.
We call it Earth.

It is the big globe,
floating in space,
on which we live.

MARS
(the next planet)
is another 140 million
miles that way →

There is much to see and do here on Earth,
so let's get started with a quick tour.

The planet is basically made up of two parts.

LAND
(ROCK and DIRT)

SEA
(WATER)

also LAND

also WATER

Firstly, let's talk about the land.
It's what we are standing on right now.
We know lots about the land.

Then, there is the sea,
which is full of wonderful things.

We're glad you found us, as space is very big.

us

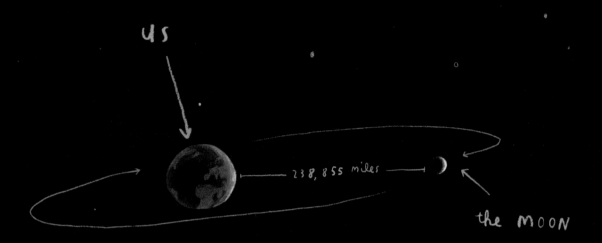

238,855 miles

the MOON

We know a bit about the sea,
but we'll talk some more about
that once you've learned to swim.

ICEBERG
(frozen water)

goes nearly
SEVEN MILES
DEEP (we think)

There is also the sky.
Though that can get pretty complicated . . .

WE SPIN AROUND the SUN

The MOON → SPINS AROUND us

OUTER SPACE

SOMETIMES the SKY IS BLUE
sometimes it's . . .

STRATOSTHINGY

WIND
(moving air)

AIR WE → BREATHE

SNOW
(FROZEN
falling water)

Rainbow

Rain
(falling
WATER)

CLOUDS
(Floating water)

LAND

THE MILKY WAY
(billions of other STARS and PLANETS)

CONSTELLATIONS
(patterns of stars)

other
Planets

STARS
(BURNING Balls
of GAS. VERY Far away
that you see at night...
unless it's RAINING.)

uh .. NOT

STORM
Clouds

lightning

OUR
ATMOSPHERE

SEA

OK, moving on.

On our planet, there are people.
One people is a person.
You are a person. You have a body.

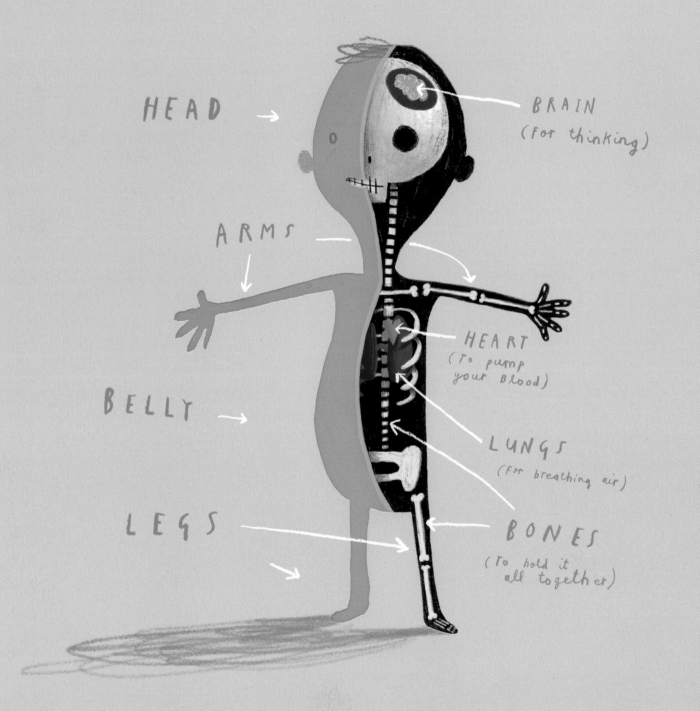

HEAD →

BRAIN
(for thinking)

ARMs

HEART
(To pump
your Blood)

BELLY →

LUNGS
(For breathing air)

LEGS

BONES
(To hold it
all together)

Look after it, as most bits
don't grow back.

Bits that GROW BACK

Nails   Hair

The most important things for people to
remember are to eat, drink and stay warm.

People come in many
shapes, sizes and colors.

We may all look different,
act different and sound different . . .

. . . but don't be fooled, we are all people.

There are animals, too. They come in even more shapes, sizes and colors.

I'm not supposed to BE HERE

They can't speak, though that's
no reason not to be nice to them.

I can!

You may not be able to speak yet either,
even though your head is filled with questions.

Be patient, you'll learn how to use words soon enough.

Generally how it works is that when the sun is out, it is daytime, and we do stuff.

The rest of the time is night when it is dark, save for the moon, and we sleep.

(Please?)

Things can sometimes move slowly here on Earth.

More often, though, they move quickly,
so use your time well.

It will be gone
before you know it.

Though we have come a long way,
we haven't quite worked everything out,
so there is plenty left for you to do.

You will figure lots of things out for yourself.
Just remember to leave notes for everyone else.

It looks big, Earth.
But there are lots of us on here

(7, 327, 450, 667 and   counting)

so be kind.

There is enough for everyone.

Well, that is Planet Earth.

Make sure you look after it,
as it's all we've got.

Now, if you need to know anything else . . .

. . . just ask.
I won't be far away.

And when I'm not around . . .

. . . you can always
ask someone else.

You're never alone on Earth.

"Looking back and seeing your planet as a planet is just an amazing feeling. It's a totally different perspective, and it makes you appreciate, actually, how fragile our existence is."

—Dr. Sally Ride, Astronaut and Physicist

"If you own an automobile, you realize that you must put oil and gas into it, and you must put water in the radiator and take care of the car as a whole. . . . You know that you're either going to have to keep the machine in good order or it's going to be in trouble and fail to function. We have not been seeing our Spaceship Earth as an integrally-designed machine which to be persistently successful must be comprehended and serviced in total."

—R. Buckminster Fuller, Inventor

"There are only three words you need to live by, son: respect, consideration and tolerance."

—Oliver's Dad, All-round good human

Thank you

Hannah Coleman, Helen Mackenzie Smith, Rory Jeffers, Michael Green,
Judith Brinsford, Anna Mitchelmore, Paul Moreton, Patrick Reynolds,
Hayley Nichols, Geraldine Stroud, Ann-Janine Murtagh, Jen Loja,
Erin Allweiss, Timothee Verrecchia, Suzanne Jeffers
and, obviously, Harland Jeffers.

Together with all those who make, sell, read and support my books.

Quotation on page 4 from J. M. Barrie's *The Little White Bird* © 1902

Extract from interview with Dr. Sally Ride reproduced by kind permission of
The American Academy of Achievement   www.achievement.org

Quote from Buckminster Fuller's *Operating Manual for Spaceship Earth* © 1969, 2008
The Estate of R. Buckminster Fuller. All rights reserved.

Philomel Books
an imprint of Penguin Random House LLC
375 Hudson Street
New York, NY 10014

Copyright © 2017 by Oliver Jeffers. First American edition published in 2017 by Philomel Books.
Published in Great Britain by HarperCollins Publishers Ltd. in 2017.
Penguin supports copyright. Copyright fuels creativity, encourages diverse voices, promotes free speech,
and creates a vibrant culture. Thank you for buying an authorized edition of this book and for complying
with copyright laws by not reproducing, scanning, or distributing any part of it in any form without
permission. You are supporting writers and allowing Penguin to continue to publish books for every reader.

Philomel Books is a registered trademark of Penguin Random House LLC.

Library of Congress Cataloging-in-Publication Data is available upon request.
Manufactured in the United States of America
ISBN 9780399167898
10 9 8 7 6 5 4 3 2 1

southern
CROSS

pointers

Achernar

SOUTH
celestial
POLE

This is
SOUTH

N
W   E
S